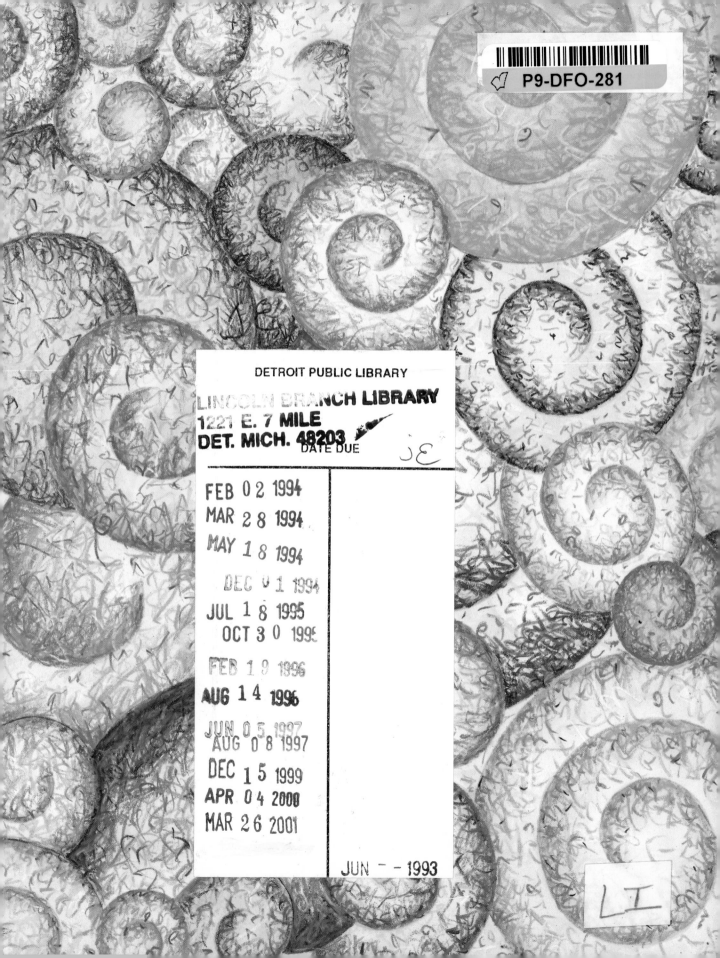

HANK'S WORK

JOSHUA SCHREIER

DUTTON CHILDREN'S BOOKS · NEW YORK

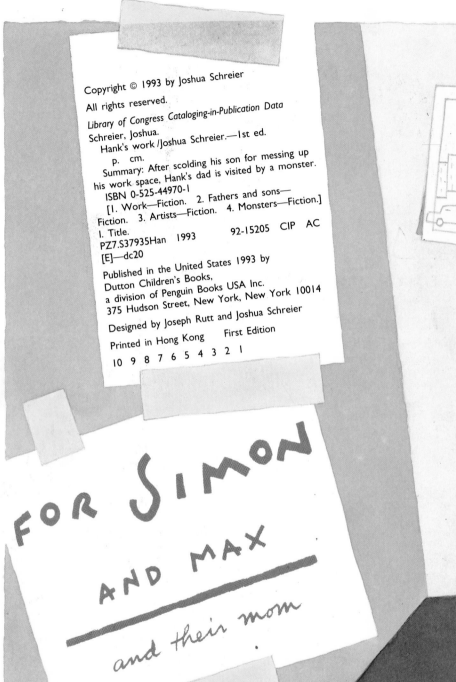

Copyright © 1993 by Joshua Schreier
Library of Congress Cataloging-in-Publication Data
Schreier, Joshua.
    Hank's work /Joshua Schreier.—1st ed.
        p.   cm.
    Summary: After scolding his son for messing up
his work space, Hank's dad is visited by a monster.
    ISBN 0-525-44970-1
    [1. Work—Fiction.   2. Fathers and sons—
Fiction.   3. Artists—Fiction.   4. Monsters—Fiction.]
I. Title.
PZ7.S37935Han   1993   92-15205 CIP AC
[E]—dc20

Published in the United States 1993 by
Dutton Children's Books,
a division of Penguin Books USA Inc.
375 Hudson Street, New York, New York 10014

Designed by Joseph Rutt and Joshua Schreier

Printed in Hong Kong   First Edition

10 9 8 7 6 5 4 3 2 1

FOR SIMON
AND MAX
and their mom

ank loved to work in his dad's studio. He especially loved to draw there. His dad's worktable was smooth and square with a special bright light. And on the table was a can full of big fat pencils in all kinds of colors.

Besides that, there were piles of paper, a cranky old pencil sharpener, paper clips, erasers, rubber stamps, scissors, a stapler, and a four-roll tape dispenser.

This morning, Hank was working very hard. He was working so hard that . . .

his dad yelled

when he walked into the studio. "I have a *lot* of work to do right now," he said, "and I can't get anything done with you rummaging around my table. Go play somewhere else. Now scram!"

"I'm *not* playing," Hank objected. "I'm *working*."
And he took some paper and pencils and stomped off
to his room.

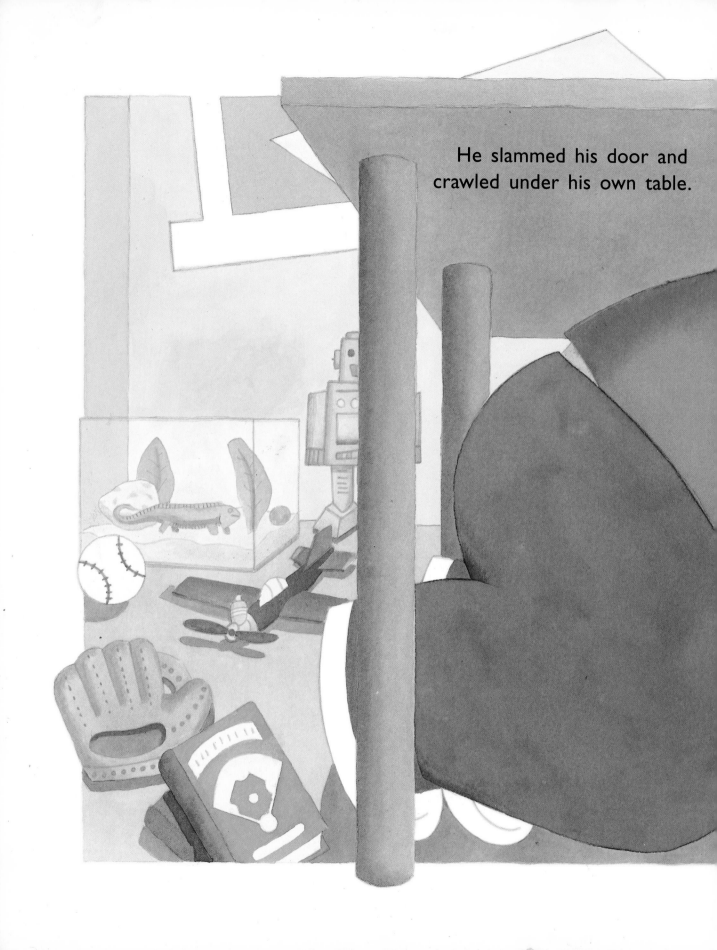

He slammed his door and crawled under his own table.

He chose an acid-green crayon
and got down to work.

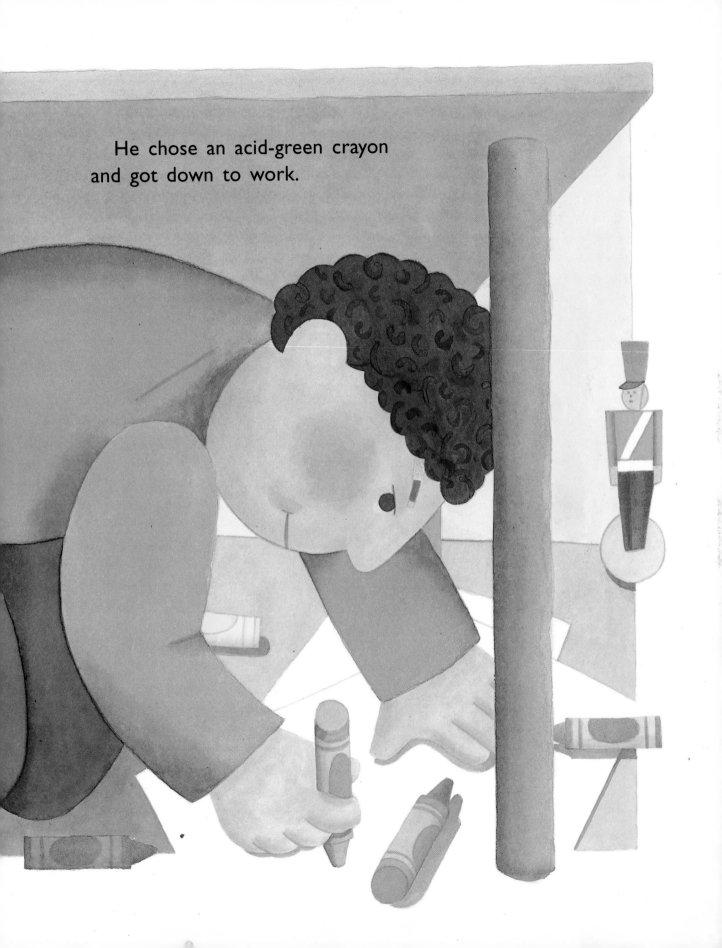

Hank drew. He drew furiously. He drew and drew.

Soon Hank's brother, Leo, woke up from his nap.
He heard a soft snort. "Nice doggie," said Leo.
Leo called anything that walked on four legs a doggie.

Right after that, in the garage, a low growl
startled Hank's mom.

"Yikes!" she gasped, but she tried to remain calm.
"Looking for someone special?" she asked.

She thought she saw a smile and a nod.

Then, in the studio, Hank's dad felt a tap on his
shoulder.

"Hank, I told you before, I don't have time to play.
Now leave me alone!"

Instead of a reply from Hank, Dad heard a low grunt.

He looked up and saw a big green face in front of him. "You're not Hank!" Dad yelled, falling back in his chair, scattering pens, pencils, and paper everywhere. "HELP!"

There was a deep green chuckle, like a voice rising from the bottom of a well. Then the voice whispered, "*Shhh,* don't yell." And suddenly everything disappeared in clouds of smoke.

"Where'd it go?"

Hank's family didn't know what was going on.

A thunderous **R-O-A-R** shook the house. Mom ran upstairs and grabbed Leo. Dad was already by Hank's door. Another **R-O-A-R** came, then silence.

In the silence, Dad muttered, "I better see if Hank's all right."

In Hank's room it was quiet. All Dad could hear was the sound of crayoning.

"Hank?" said his father, softly. "Are you okay? There seems to be some sort of monster in the house. Did you see it?"

For a while, Hank didn't say anything. He kept on coloring. Finally he said, "You yelled at me. I don't like yelling. Monsters don't either."

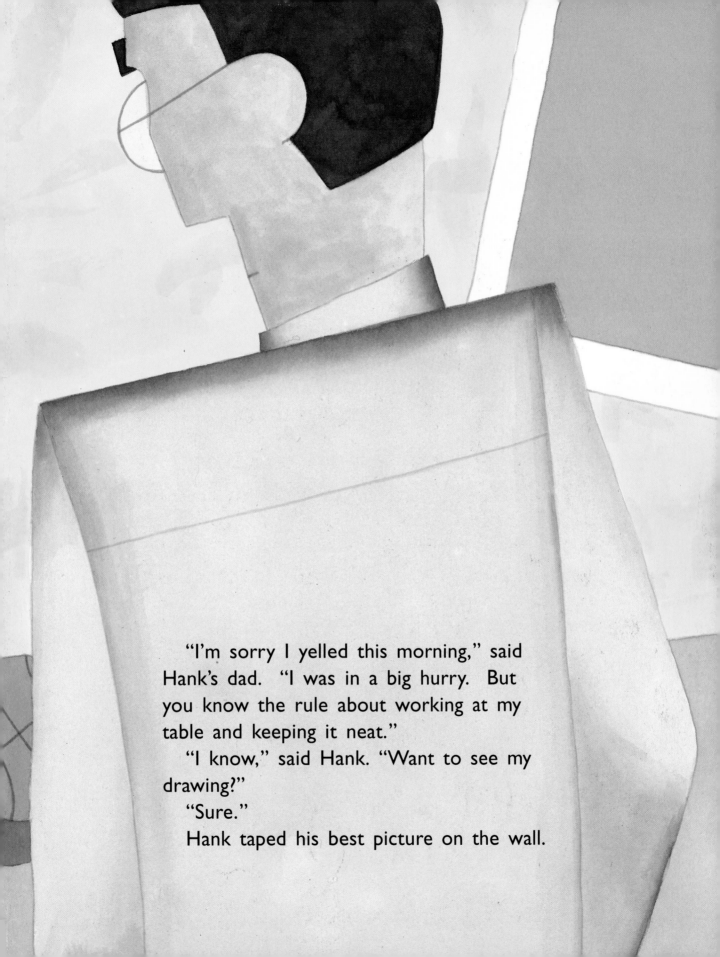

"I'm sorry I yelled this morning," said Hank's dad. "I was in a big hurry. But you know the rule about working at my table and keeping it neat."

"I know," said Hank. "Want to see my drawing?"

"Sure."

Hank taped his best picture on the wall.

His dad looked at it very carefully.
"Good work, Hank," he said. "Good work."
Hank just smiled.

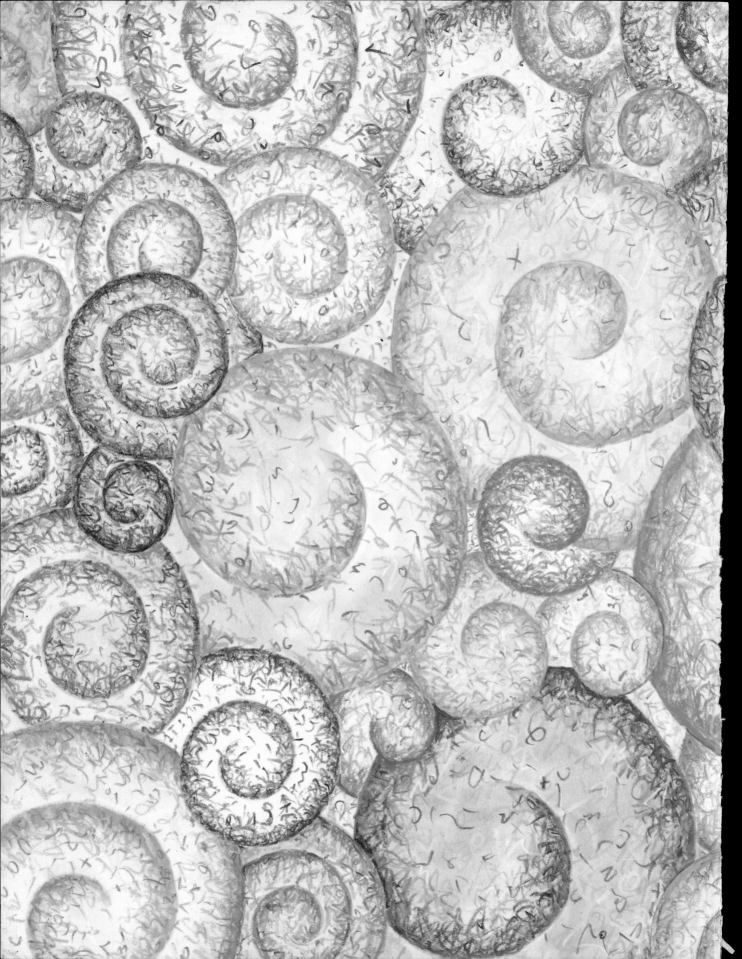